MY PERFECT PUP

For Pippy and Scruff. SW

To Bekir, my perfect puppy ...
in a kitten body! AT

First published in the UK in 2018.
This edition published in 2018
by New Frontier Publishing Europe Ltd
93 Harbord Street, London SW6 6PN
www.newfrontierpublishing.co.uk

ISBN: 978-1-912076-81-9 (PB)

A CIP catalogue record for this book is available from
the British Library.

Printed in China
10 9 8 7 6 5 4 3 2 1

MY PERFECT PUP

Sue Walker
Illustrated by Anil Tortop

NEW FRONTIER PUBLISHING

The moment Milly and Max entered the pet shop, the tiniest pup was on his very best behaviour.

'I want a pretty pup,' said Milly.
'So I can brush it, and primp it, and preen it.'

'I want a clever pup,'
said Max.
'So it can learn tricks
and ride in the basket
on our bicycle.'

'Walk this way,' said the pet shop owner. 'I'm sure we'll have the perfect pup for you.'

Poodle pups yipped, and Boxer pups yapped,
Bully pups nipped, and Scotty pups snapped,

Collie pups bounced, and Pointer pups pounced,
but the tiniest pup waited politely.

'You're perfect,' said Milly,
when she spied his long lashes.

The tiniest pup sniffed and licked
and wagged and rolled.

Then Max said, 'Look!
I didn't even ask him to sit.'

So quite soon, they took him home on their tandem.

'Let's call him Tiny,' said Milly, and Max agreed.

But the trouble was ...

Tiny didn't stay tiny for long.
And what's more, he didn't stay pretty either.

Tiny hated brushing, and primping, and preening

and Max's tricks were always
just a little too tricky.

So one day Milly and Max told Tiny,
'We're sorry, but you're not our perfect pup after all.'
And they took Tiny all the way back to the pet shop.

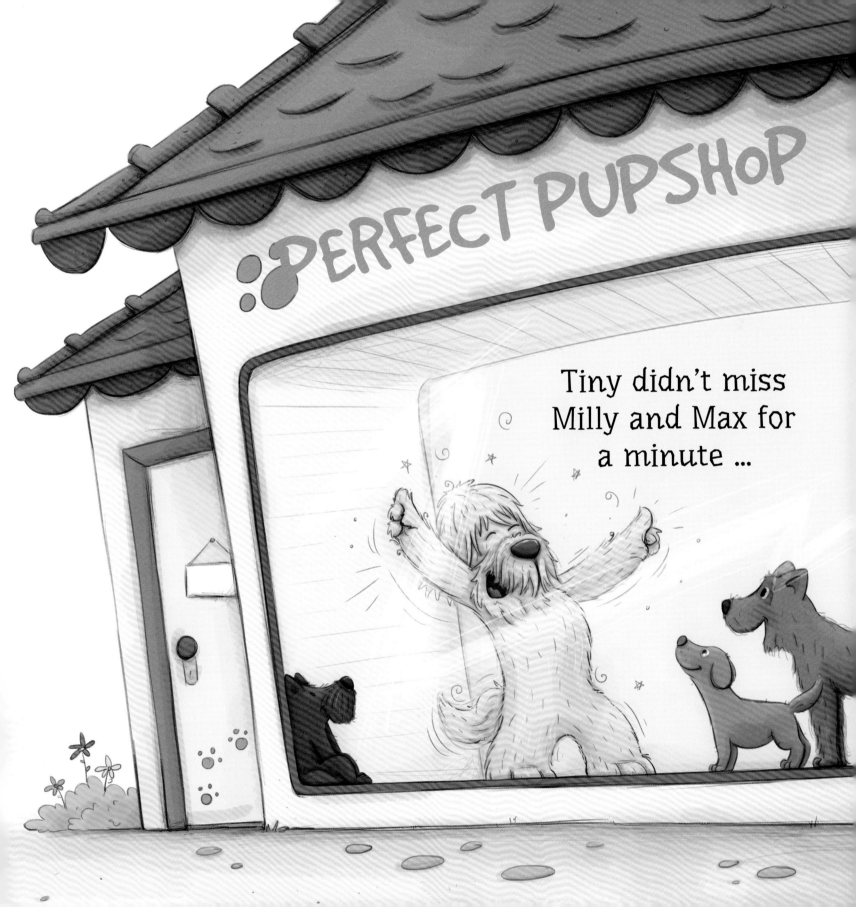

Tiny didn't miss
Milly and Max for
a minute ...

because he was much too busy choosing a friend.

Too prissy,

too mean.

Too quiet,

too keen.

Too bossy, too grim. Too clever, too prim.

So when Joe Barnaby arrived, Tiny knew ...

Joe was definitely the right boy for him.

And right then, Joe took Tiny home in his dad's truck.

Tiny was as big as a horse.
So that's what Joe Barnaby named him.

Horse learned to stand,

and stop,

and lie down

and he always came when Joe Barnaby called him.
Joe never once brushed him, or primped him,
or preened him.

Horse was a sheep dog.
And sometimes in the evenings,
Horse ...

was a horse dog.

'Giddy-up,' said Joe Barnaby's baby brother as
they rode around the yard, through the barn and
all the way up the stairs.

And as they snuggled down into bed,
Joe always whispered, 'You're the perfect pup,
Horse Barnaby.'
And Horse knew
he had found the perfect family too.